This book belongs to:

. . . .

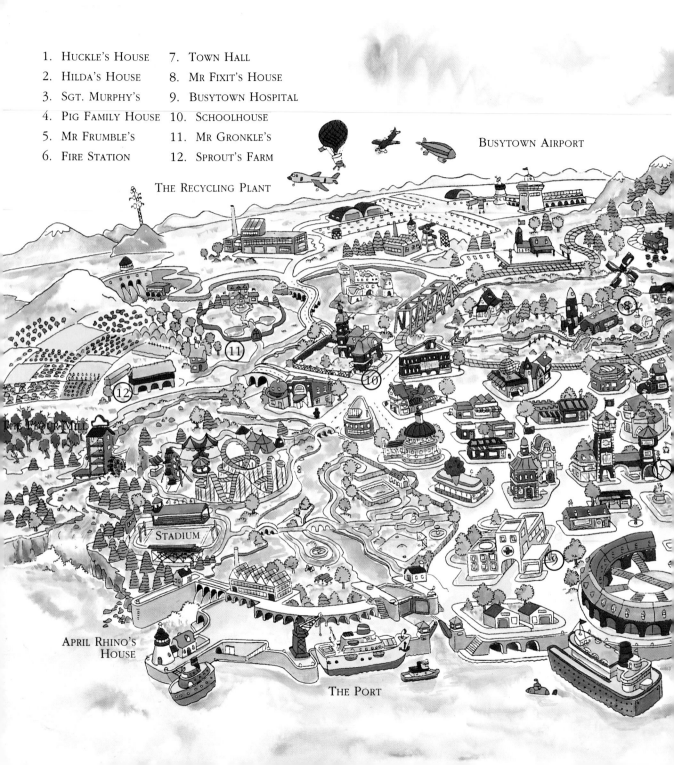

The Recycling Plant

Busytown Airport

The Flour Mill

Stadium

April Rhino's House

The Port

First published in Great Britain in 1994
by HarperCollins Publishers Ltd,
77-85 Fulham Palace Road,
Hammersmith, London W6 8JB
10 9 8 7 6 5 4 3 2 1
Copyright © 1994 the Estate of Richard Scarry
Adapted from the animated television series
The Busy World of Richard Scarry (TM)
produced by Paramount Pictures and Cinar
All rights reserved.
ISBN: 0 00 664552 6
Printed and bound in Italy
Designed and produced by Les Livres du Dragon d'Or.

The Busy World of Richard Scarry

A Big Operation

Collins

An Imprint of HarperCollins*Publishers*

Huckle doesn't feel very well this morning.
He has a sore throat. Dr Lion has come to examine him.
He listens to Huckle's heartbeat.
"How does it sound, Dr Lion?" Lowly asks.
"Hmmm, you have a fever, Huckle. And this is your third
sore throat this year, isn't it," remarks Dr Lion.

"I think Huckle should have his tonsils taken out," Dr Lion says.
"Does that mean he has to go to the hospital?" Mother Cat is worried and so is Huckle.
"You're not scared are you, Huckle?" Sally asks.
"Oh, no!" says Huckle. His voice is very hoarse.

"Don't worry, Huckle," says Dr Lion. "I'll take you and your family on a grand tour of the hospital before we check you in."

The hospital is a very busy place.
Look! Here comes an ambulance!
"Stand aside, everyone!" call the ambulance men.
"It's an emergency!"

It's Mr Frumble!
"Oh, good morning, Mr Frumble," says Nurse Nora. "We've reserved your usual room."
"Hello, Nurse Nora," Mr Frumble answers. "I'm afraid I fell on my nose again, chasing my hat."
"Well, I'm glad you found it," says Nurse Nora.

Dr Lion takes the Cat Family
on a tour of the hospital.
First they visit the operating
room.

Just look at all that equipment!

Huckle, Sally and Lowly are impressed.

Then Dr Lion takes them to another room.
"This is the X-Ray Department," he announces.
They enter the darkened room.

"Yikes!" Sally shouts. "They've got skeletons in here!"
"They are not spooky skeletons, Sally," Dr Lion explains.

"These are x-ray pictures of patients who are treated in the hospital. People like Mr Frumble."

"Look, here's Mr Frumble's broken nose!"

"Can we borrow this machine for Halloween?" asks Sally.
"I don't think so, Sally," Dr Lion answers.

Dr Lion takes them outside
into the garden.
"Hospitals aren't so bad
after all," Huckle says.
"I'll have the operation, but
can Lowly stay with me?"
        "Of course he can,"
        says Dr Lion.
        "We will have such
        fun!" Lowly exclaims.

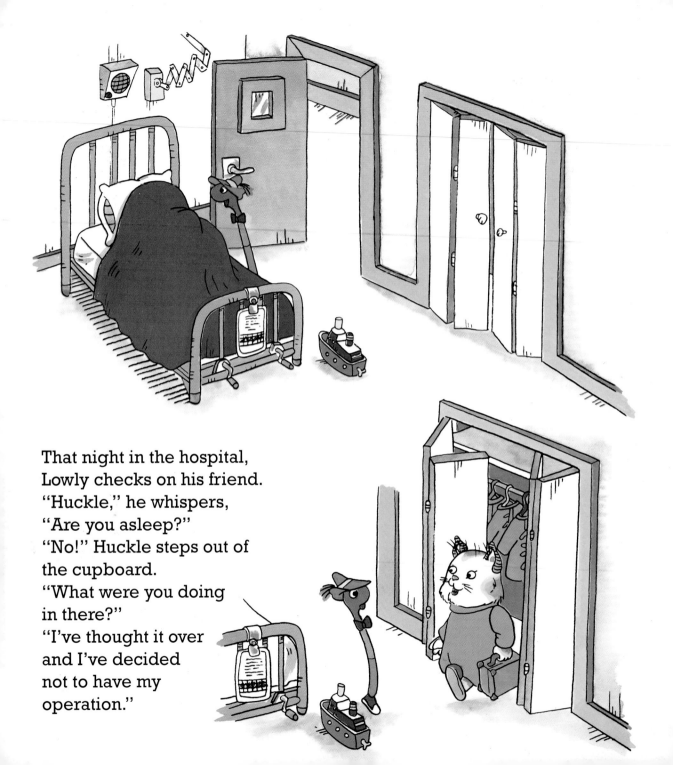

That night in the hospital,
Lowly checks on his friend.
"Huckle," he whispers,
"Are you asleep?"
"No!" Huckle steps out of
the cupboard.
"What were you doing
in there?"
"I've thought it over
and I've decided
not to have my
operation."

Huckle leaves the room,
taking his suitcase with him.
"Huckle, are you leaving
because you're scared?"
Lowly asks.
"Scared? Me? Ha!" laughs
Huckle. "Well, maybe just
a little..."

"Listen, Huckle. I have an idea. Maybe if you talk to
some of the other patients you will feel a bit better.
Let's go and see Sprout Goat."

"Hi, Sprout. Why are *you* in hospital?"
Huckle asks.

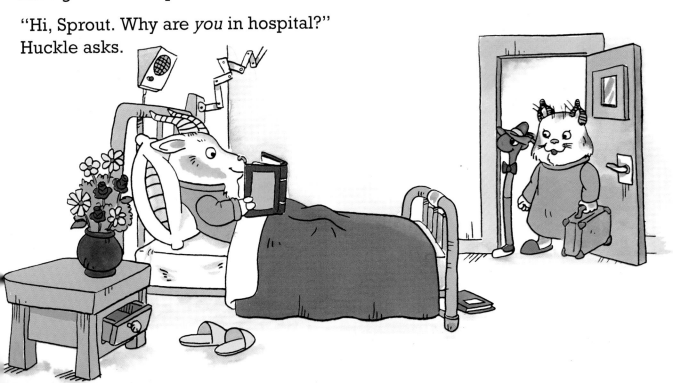

"I'm here for another operation to straighten my leg. It's the fourth and last time," Sprout explains.
"You've been here four times and you're not scared!" Huckle is amazed.

"I was at first, but the nurses are so nice..."
"But don't the operations hurt?"
"A little bit, afterwards," Sprout says, "but you sleep right through the operation and don't feel a thing."

"What are *you* in for?"
Sprout asks Huckle.
"To have my tonsils out."
"Oh! You are lucky!"
exclaims Sprout. "After
the operation, you will
get ALL the ice cream
you can eat!"
"Wow!" says Lowly.
"Ice cream sounds good,
but I'm still leaving,"
says Huckle.

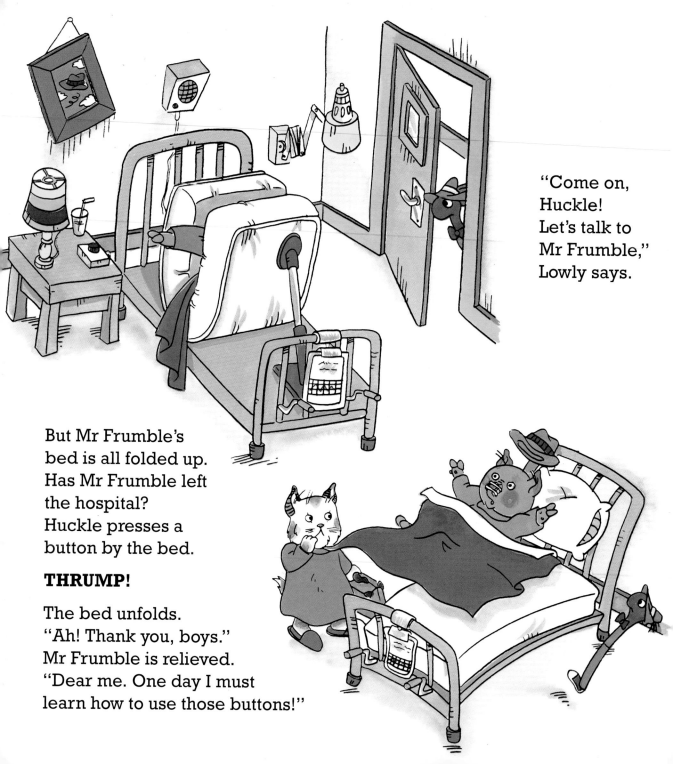

"Come on, Huckle! Let's talk to Mr Frumble," Lowly says.

But Mr Frumble's bed is all folded up. Has Mr Frumble left the hospital? Huckle presses a button by the bed.

THRUMP!

The bed unfolds. "Ah! Thank you, boys." Mr Frumble is relieved. "Dear me. One day I must learn how to use those buttons!"

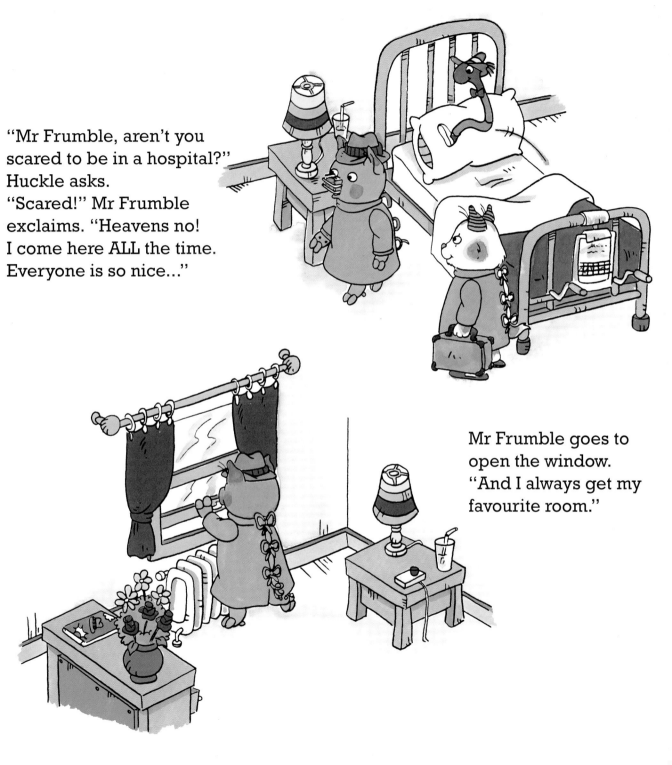

"Mr Frumble, aren't you scared to be in a hospital?" Huckle asks.
"Scared!" Mr Frumble exclaims. "Heavens no! I come here ALL the time. Everyone is so nice..."

Mr Frumble goes to open the window. "And I always get my favourite room."

"Sprout and Mr Frumble need to be in hospital. They have real problems. All I have is a little sore throat," says Huckle. "I'm leaving!"

Just then, Huckle sees a friend of his. "Oh, Mrs Stitches! What's wrong with you?" he asks.
"Nothing at all, boys. I have a new baby and this hospital is taking the BEST care of both of us."

Nurse Nancy comes in holding Mrs Stitches' new baby. The baby giggles in the nurse's arms. "Well!" Lowly exclaims. "SHE certainly looks happy to be here." "Hmmm..." says Huckle, thoughtfully. "If a little baby isn't afraid to be here, I guess I shouldn't be either!"

Huckle decides to go back to his room.

The next morning, Huckle is brought to the operating room.

He is very quiet.

Dr Lion takes out a mask and says to Huckle, "Try to count backwards from one hundred."

"OK," Huckle says and he begins to count:
"One hundred, ninety nine, ninety eleven, ninety eight...mmm...mm..."
In a moment, the special gas has put Huckle to sleep.

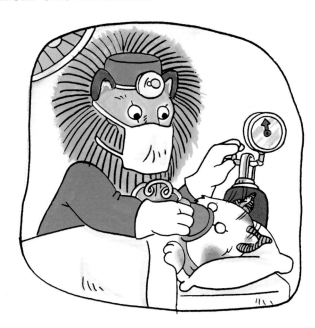

"Huckle? Huckle, are you all
right?" Sally asks.
Huckle slowly opens his eyes and
whispers, "Ninety seven... Hey!"
He looks around at his friends.
"What are you all doing here?"
"The operation is over," Father Cat
says. "You have been asleep
for hours..."
"How do you feel, darling?"
Mother Cat asks.
"My throat is still sore,"
Huckle replies.

"Hey, Huckle! How about a little ice cream?" suggests Lowly, jumping on the bed.

Huckle takes a spoonful and swallows. Ow! It hurts!

"Hey, Sprout. You said I could have all the ice cream I can eat!" Huckle protests.

"No, I said all the ice cream you *could* eat!" says Sprout. "But I can see you can't eat any just yet!"

"Well," says Lowly, taking Huckle's spoon, "if I ever have MY tonsils out...

...you can eat all MY ice cream. I promise!''

1. HUCKLE'S HOUSE
2. HILDA'S HOUSE
3. SGT. MURPHY'S
4. PIG FAMILY HOUSE
5. MR FRUMBLE'S
6. FIRE STATION
7. TOWN HALL
8. MR FIXIT'S HOUSE
9. BUSYTOWN HOSPITAL
10. SCHOOLHOUSE
11. MR GRONKLE'S
12. SPROUT'S FARM

BUSYTOWN AIRPORT

THE RECYCLING PLANT

STADIUM

APRIL RHINO'S
HOUSE

THE PORT